Happy Birthday Mill - 11
Love Aunty K

MW01142309

If You Cuddle With A Crocodile

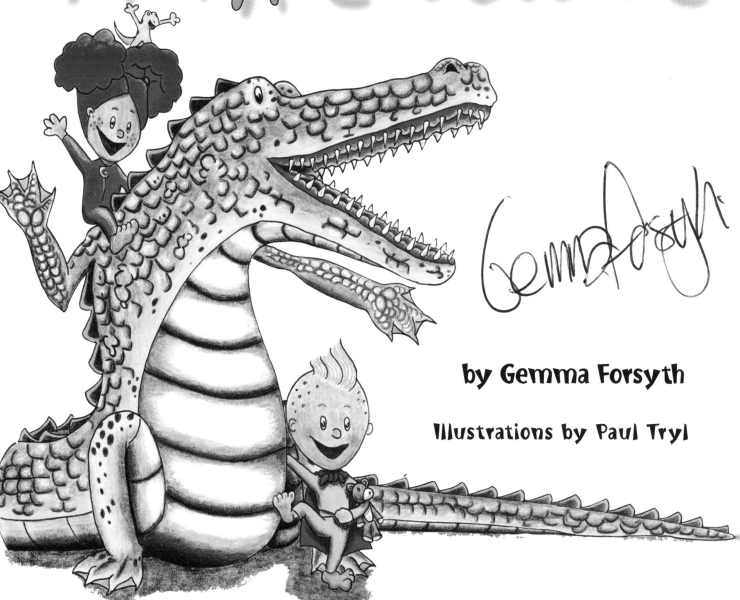

by Gemma Forsyth

Illustrations by Paul Tryl

Mystic Lights Publishing

Mystic Lights Publishing
West 4th Ave RPO
P.O. Box 19173
Vancouver, BC, Canada
V6K 4R8

ISBN: 978-0-9784986-5-8

Illustrations by Paul Tryl

Book Design by Julius Kiskis

21 20 19 18 17 16 15 14 13   1 2 3 4 5

Dedication

For my two beautiful daughters,
Daisy and Violet.
My deepest appreciation to Michael O'Brien,
Suzanne O'Brien, Julius Kiskis, Mystic Lights
Publishing and my sisters, Sage and Chance
for making this book possible.
Also to my family and friends
for their love and support.
And a special "thank you" to Paul Tryl
for his brilliant co-creation of this book
as well as our two daughters.

If you want to get to sleep tonight and you're looking for something new.
Here's some friendly advice, some things I've tried, that might be right for you.

The snoring from an
elephant's trunk is not as
bad as you might think.
But they ALWAYS insist on
the top bunk, which tends
to make it sink.

I thought a moose might be kind of fun but
he barely fit through the door.

And with those HUGE antlers and such LONG legs,
there's only room for you on the floor.

I decided to
try something
smaller, so
I invited in
some sheep . . .

but sheep like to stay up counting themselves instead of going to sleep.

You may want to stick with a teddy, rather than a grizzly bear.
Their breath is REALLY stinky and they put honey in your hair!

Snakes hog all the covers.

Pigs can be quite rough. They snort and grunt and kick and push AND play with all your stuff.

If you cuddle with a crocodile you're assured sweet lullabies.
But if asked to stop after 100 or so, crocodiles usually start to cry.

You better get some earplugs,
you'll need your own life jacket.
Their tears can add up really fast
and their sobs make quite a racket!

Gorillas tell great bedtime stories
about pirates and fairies and elves . . .

**but they REALLY, REALLY like to hug,
and won't sleep by themselves.**

When giraffes get a case of the giggles, it lasts throughout the night.
Cheetahs are restless sleepers, keep your pillows out of sight.

Bats like to turn on the ceiling fan
and hang there by their toes.

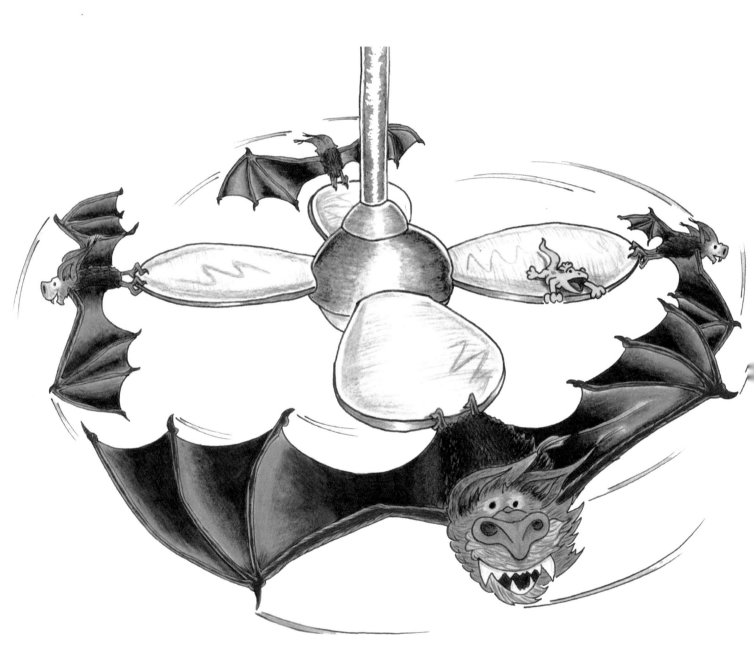

They take turns spinning around
and around, then landing on your nose!

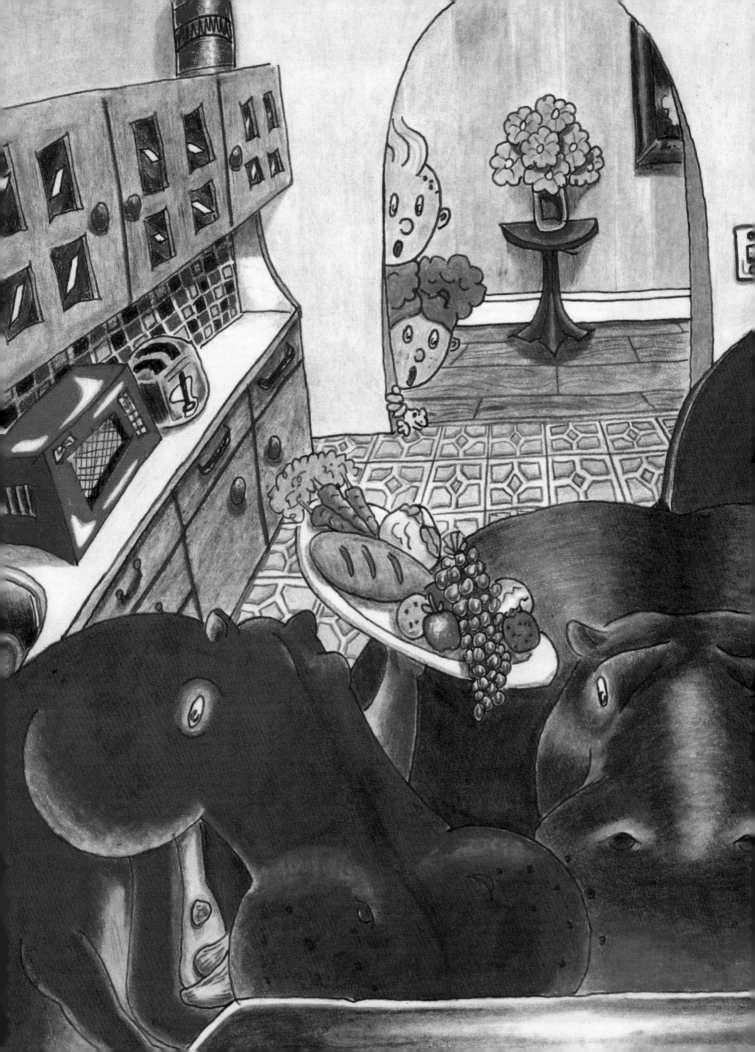

Hippos make wonderful house guests. They're polite and kind and sweet, but you better fill up the refrigerator cause MAN do they love to eat!

They also stay awake all night
and talk about their day.
They chew and slurp and crunch
AND have an awful lot to say.

Cozy up with a pack
of wolves, it will help
you drift off soon . . .
that is unless, as you
may have guessed,
it's the night
of a full moon.

Rhinos won't share anything . . .

Lions never
brush their
teeth . . .

Tigers always whine and pout
until they're rocked to sleep.

So my friends,
in the end,
to get the
perfect rest . . .
a blanket, a
buddy, and a
good-night kiss
is what I
think is best.

THE

END

CPSIA information can be obtained
at www.ICGtesting.com
Printed in the USA
LVIW02n0822151213
364898LV00001B/2